Super-Secret
Valentine

Super-Secret Valentine

by ABBY KLEIN

illustrated by JOHN MCKINLEY

THE BLUE SKY PRESS
An Imprint of Scholastic Inc. • New York

To my Super-Secret Valentine—J.K.
Love you forever . . . Smoochie,
A.K.

THE BLUE SKY PRESS

Text copyright © 2007 by Abby Klein
Illustrations copyright © 2007 by John McKinley
All rights reserved.

Special thanks to Robert Martin Staenberg.

No part of this publication may be reproduced, stored in
a retrieval system, or transmitted in any form or by any means,
electronic, mechanical, photocopying, recording, or otherwise,
without written permission of the publisher. For information
regarding permission, please write to: Permissions Department,
Scholastic Inc., 557 Broadway, New York, New York 10012.
SCHOLASTIC, THE BLUE SKY PRESS, and associated logos are
trademarks and/or registered trademarks of Scholastic Inc.
Library of Congress catalog card number: 2006014836
ISBN 10: 0-439-78459-X / ISBN 13: 978-0-439-78459-7
10 9 8 7 6 5 4 3 2   07 08 09 10 11
Printed in the United States of America   40
First printing, January 2007

CHAPTERS

I have a problem.

A really, really, big problem.

I want to give Jessie a special

valentine for Valentine's Day,

but I don't want anyone

else to know.

Let me tell you about it.

CHAPTER 1

The Chase

"AHHHHH! HELP! HELP!" Chloe screamed as she raced around the playground, waving her arms wildly in the air. "He's gonna get me! He's gonna get me!"

As I peeked around the side of the building where I was hiding, I saw Max, the biggest bully in the whole first grade, chasing her. I turned to my best friend, Robbie. "At least he's not chasing us right now," I whispered. "This is a good hiding place."

"Yeah," said Robbie. "He'll never find us back here. We're safe."

Just as he said that, Chloe ran right past us, and Max discovered our secret hiding place. "There you two wimps are," he said, grinning. "I've been looking all over for you."

I gulped. Great. Just great.

"I'd start running if I were you," said Max.

Robbie and I took off like lightning. We ran through the basketball courts, across the grass, and under the slide, with Max right at our heels. "You guys are never going to get away this time!" Max yelled.

It felt as if we had been running forever. My heart was beating so fast, I thought it would explode. Didn't this guy ever get tired? Every recess he chased us all over the playground.

"Hurry up, Freddy," Robbie called. "He's catching up. Don't slow down now."

I could feel Max's hot breath on my neck.

He reached out to grab my shirt and got a small piece of it, but I yanked my body away, made a quick turn, and started running in the opposite direction. As Max turned to see where I was going, he accidentally knocked into Chloe, who was still running for her life. He sent her sailing onto the pavement.

"OWWWW! OWWWWW!" Chloe wailed, grabbing her knee. "I'm bleeding! Help me! I'm bleeding!"

We stopped running and gathered around her to see what all the crying was about.

"Look what you did, you big meanie," she screamed at Max. "My tights are ripped, my party dress is dirty, and my new shoes have scratches all over them. Do you know how much these shoes cost? They are very expensive. You are in big trouble!"

"Maybe you shouldn't wear such fancy shoes to school," Max snarled.

Just then our teacher, Mrs. Wushy, came running over.

"Oh my goodness!" she said. "Chloe, what happened to you?"

"I'll tell you what happened," Chloe sobbed, pointing to Max. "That big bully over there was chasing me, and he knocked me over."

Mrs. Wushy turned to Max. "Is that true, Max? Did you push Chloe?"

"Well . . . um," he stammered.

"Max, I asked you a question. I'm waiting for an answer," Mrs. Wushy continued.

"I . . . uh . . . I . . . uh."

"Max Sellars, if you don't answer me this instant, then you are going to go sit on the bench over there until you have an answer."

"It was an accident."

"No it wasn't!" Chloe screamed. "He pushed me. He's lying."

"I didn't push you, you little fancy pants,"

said Max. "I was chasing Freddy, and I bumped into you by accident."

"And he was chasing me, too," Chloe whined. "Like he does every recess."

"Max," said Mrs. Wushy, "were you chasing kids again?"

"I just bumped into her by accident."

"Liar!" Chloe cried. "You're a big, fat liar!"

"All right, Chloe. That's enough," said Mrs. Wushy. She turned back to Max. "But if you weren't chasing kids, then accidents like this wouldn't happen. Right? What is the rule about chasing?"

"No chasing allowed," Max mumbled.

"What's that? I didn't hear you," said Mrs. Wushy. "Please look at me when you speak."

"No chasing allowed," Max grouched.

"That's right. I don't like you chasing other children because somebody always ends up getting hurt."

I poked Robbie in the side and whispered, "He never gets hurt. Only the rest of us."

The bell rang, signaling the end of recess.

"Well, Max," said Mrs. Wushy, "this recess is over. It looks as if you are going to have to sit on the bench at lunch recess."

"What?" Max protested. "That's not fair!"

"Oh, I think it's very fair. You need to start remembering the rules. Maybe sitting on the bench will give you some time to think."

Mrs. Wushy reached her hand out to Chloe to help her up. "Come on, Chloe, honey. Let's go inside and get you cleaned up."

"But what about my brand-new shoes?" she whimpered. "They're ruined."

"We'll see what we can do about those, too. When I'm done, you won't see a scratch."

As the rest of us went to get in line, Max came up behind me and whispered in my ear, "It's all your fault. I'm gonna get you for this."

CHAPTER 2

Valentines Are
for Everyone

After we all came back to the room from recess, Mrs. Wushy washed off Chloe's knee and put a Band-Aid on it. Then Chloe limped over to the rug to sit down.

"Excuse me, Mrs. Wushy. I don't know if I can bend this knee to sit down."

"Waa, waa, waa . . . She is such a drama queen," I whispered to Jessie. "She is always whining about something."

"I know," Jessie whispered back. "The way she's acting, you'd think she broke her leg."

Jessie never whines or complains. She is one of the toughest kids in the class. In fact, she is one of the few kids who stands up to Max. She isn't afraid of him at all. I wish I could be more like Jessie. I like her a lot. She is a really good friend.

Just then, Max's voice interrupted my thoughts. "Oh, just sit down, you little baby!" he yelled at Chloe. "It's just a little scrape."

"It is not little at all. It's huge," she said. "For your information, mister, it was bleeding all over the place."

"Bleeding all over the place?" Robbie whispered. "What planet is she living on? I think I saw two drops of blood."

Jessie, Robbie, and I started to giggle.

"Stop laughing at me!" Chloe said, pouting. "It's not funny. It really hurts."

"OK. That's enough, everyone," said Mrs. Wushy. "Chloe, I think you're going to be fine. If you don't think you can sit on the rug right now, then just sit in a chair, and put your leg out straight."

Chloe pulled out a chair and slowly sat down. She stuck her sore leg straight out in front of her.

Max spun around. "Hey, watch it, you little priss. You just kicked me in the back."

"I did not. I was just sticking my leg out like Mrs. Wushy told me to do."

Max started to push Chloe's leg back.

"Stop it! Stop it! You're hurting me!" she cried. "You're hurting me!"

Mrs. Wushy ran over and stood in between the two of them. "I don't want to hear another word out of either of you. Max, you need to go find another spot on the rug."

"But . . . why me?" he groaned.

"Because I said so," Mrs. Wushy answered. "I want the two of you as far away from each other as possible."

"How about moving her to another class?" Max said, pointing to Chloe. "That's pretty far away . . . but not far enough."

Now Mrs. Wushy was really angry. You could almost see the steam coming out of her ears. "One more word out of you, Max, and you'll be going to see Mr. Pendergast."

Mr. Pendergast is our principal. Max had actually been to see him a few times. Luckily, I had never been sent to the principal's office. It was not a place you wanted to go.

Max found a seat at the front of the rug and finally decided to keep his mouth shut.

"Well, boys and girls," said Mrs. Wushy, "I'm glad to see that everyone is ready to listen now, because we have some very important business to discuss. Does anyone know what special day it is on Friday?"

Robbie's hand shot up. He is a genius. He knows all the answers.

"Yes, Robbie?" said Mrs. Wushy.

"Friday is Valentine's Day."

"That's right."

"I just love Valentine's Day," Jessie whispered in my ear.

"Me, too," I whispered back.

"On Valentine's Day," Mrs. Wushy went on, "we are going to have a little party, and you can all pass out valentines to your friends."

"Cool," I said. Next to Christmas, I think Valentine's Day is my favorite holiday.

Chloe raised her hand. "Excuse me, Mrs. Wushy. I have a question."

"Yes, Chloe?"

"So, for the party we only have to make valentines for our friends, right?"

"That's a good question. No. You need to make one for everyone in the class."

"But you said that we were going to pass out valentines to our friends. Not everyone in this class is my friend," she said, glaring at Max.

"That's not true," said Mrs. Wushy. "We are all friends in this class."

"B-b-but," Chloe stammered.

I agreed with Chloe on this one. I wasn't too excited about making a valentine for Max.

"No 'buts,' Chloe. I make the rules, and I say that you have to make a valentine for everyone. You cannot pick and choose. Does anyone know why I made this rule?"

Robbie raised his hand again.

"Yes, Robbie, what do you think?"

"I think you made the rule because you didn't want anyone's feelings to get hurt."

"That is exactly right," said Mrs. Wushy, smiling. "Chloe, how do you think you would

feel if Robbie got twenty valentines, and you only got three?"

"Three?" Chloe laughed. "I would get way more than three."

"Three?" I whispered to Jessie. "She'd be lucky if she got that many. She should be glad that Mrs. Wushy has that rule."

"Well, this way I know no one will be left out," said Mrs. Wushy. "So if you don't count yourself, you need to bring in nineteen

valentines on Friday. I wrote everyone's name down on this note for your parents. You can check the names off as you go, and that way you'll know you've made one for everybody in the class."

Jessie raised her hand. "Can we put candy in the envelopes?"

"Yes, Jessie, you can put a little piece of candy in your valentine if it's OK with your parents. Just check with them first."

My eyes got big just thinking about all that yummy candy.

"Any other questions? Yes, Freddy."

"What are we going to put all of our valentines in?"

"That's a great question," said Mrs. Wushy. "Tomorrow we are going to decorate special bags to collect all of the valentines."

"How about treats?" Max blurted out. "How can you have a party without treats?"

"Max," said Mrs. Wushy, "you need to remember to raise your hand and not just call out. To answer your question, we will be having some treats on Friday. I'm not going to tell you right now. I'll let it be a surprise."

"I love surprises," Jessie whispered.

"Me, too!" I said, smiling at her.

This was going to be the best Valentine's Day ever. I was going to surprise Jessie with the biggest, best valentine she ever saw!

CHAPTER 3

Crooked Hearts

Usually we buy our valentines at the store, but this year my mom and my sister, Suzie, decided they wanted to make valentines. My mom had bought red and pink paper, stickers, glitter, markers, stamps, and doilies.

"All this stuff is for girls," I groaned. "How am I going to make my valentines?"

"Well, I thought you could cut out a big red heart, put one of these cool shark stickers on it, and write 'Happy Valentine's Day,'" said my mom.

"That's going to take forever. Why couldn't we just buy them like we always do?"

"Stop your complaining, you little pain," said Suzie. "Mom got some really awesome stuff. This is going to be so much fun!"

"Maybe for you, but not for me. I don't even know how to cut out a heart!"

"Don't worry, honey," said my mom. "I'll help you. They're going to be beautiful."

"Beautiful is for girls," I said. "I want mine to look cool."

"Then we'll make them look cool. Here, cut out this heart I traced," my mom said as she handed me a piece of paper.

I reached for a pair of scissors, but Suzie pushed my hand away and grabbed them first. "Those are mine, Shark Breath!" she yelled.

"Suzie, there is no reason to fight. I bought all of these things for you two to share. There is plenty of stuff here for both of you."

"Well, these are *my* scissors. The little baby can use that pair over there."

"Whatever, Brat," I said, sticking my tongue out at her.

"Enough, you two," said my mom. "Do you think we can do this without fighting? This is supposed to be fun."

Neither one of us answered.

"Well?"

"Yeah, I guess," I said.

"Thank you very much, Freddy. Now how about you, Suzie?"

"Yeah."

"Great. Now, Freddy, just cut right on that line I drew."

I tried to cut carefully, but the heart came out all crooked. I crumpled it up and threw it on the floor.

"Freddy, what are you doing?" asked my mom. "Why did you just crumple it up?"

"That one was all crooked. I told you that I can't cut a heart!"

"Oh, now you're just being silly. Of course you can cut a heart. Here. Try again."

She handed me another heart, and I tried to cut even slower this time but I messed up again. "There. You see? It's all crooked," I said, shoving it in my mom's face.

"No, it's not. It's just fine. You're being too hard on yourself. Now why don't you choose one of these stickers to put on it?"

Sharks are my favorite animal, and my mom had found some really great shark stickers for me to put on my valentines. "These are cool, Mom. My friends are going to love them."

"I know. Aren't they great? I thought of you the minute I saw them."

Suzie looked up from the valentines she was making. "Sharks, sharks, sharks!" she

moaned. "You know, you are a shark freak. You have to dress up as a shark every Halloween. Every T-shirt you have has to have a shark on it. You're always rubbing that stupid shark's tooth for good luck. Ugh!"

"My shark's tooth is not stupid, and it does bring me good luck!"

"So what if Freddy likes sharks?" said my mom. "What's wrong with that?"

"Yeah," I said. "What's wrong with that?"

"Well, if you like them so much, maybe you should marry them," Suzie teased.

"Well, since you like the bathroom so much, maybe you should marry it!"

"Stop it, you two!" yelled my mom. "If you can't get along, then we just won't make any more valentines."

"But I have to make one for everyone in my class. That's the rule."

"Then I suggest the two of you leave each other alone," said my mom.

"Fine," I mumbled. "Now what do I have to do next?"

"You just have to write the person's name at the top, use this stamp that says, 'Happy Valentine's Day,' and then sign your name."

"That's going to take forever!"

"It will if you keep complaining instead of working," said my mom. "If you just do it, you'll see it won't take very long, and you'll have fun doing it."

"Oh, all right," I said.

I got to work, and before I realized it, I had made eighteen valentines. "You were right, Mom. This is a lot of fun."

"Yeah," said Suzie. "I love making my own valentines. This glitter is really sparkly. Thanks for buying it, Mom."

"Remember, I told you that glitter makes a mess. You are only allowed to use it in the kitchen when I'm around."

My mom is such a Neat Freak. She is always afraid that we are going to spill something. We can't take food out of the kitchen, and all

art projects have to be done at the kitchen table, so we don't get glue on the rug.

"I know, I know," said Suzie.

The only valentine I had left to make was the super-special one for Jessie. I reached for a big piece of red paper and the glitter.

"What are you doing?" asked Suzie. "Making one for your girlfriend?"

"What? I don't have a girlfriend."

"He must be making one for Jessie," said my mom. "That's the only name he hasn't checked off the list."

Great! Just great! Did she have to say that?

"I knew it," said Suzie, snickering. "Maybe you want to put some extra glitter on that one and give it a little kiss."

I could feel my face turning bright red. "This one is not for Jessie," I lied. "I was making it for Mom. I thought I was done with all the ones for my class."

"Oh, Freddy, that is so sweet," said my mom, giving me a hug.

"I'll just make Jessie's, and then I'll finish yours, Mom."

There was no way I could make Jessie's extra-special valentine here in front of Suzie.

She would never stop teasing me. Right now, I was going to have to make Jessie one like I did for the rest of the class, and then later I would have to make the super-secret valentine in my room when no one was looking.

The only problem was going to be sneaking all the supplies up to my room. I would have to make a plan, but I needed some help.

I could ask my best friend, Robbie, to help me. He always had really good ideas. One time he helped me sneak some garlic powder out of the kitchen when I was trying to get rid of a vampire. Another time, we snuck outside in the middle of the night to look for nocturnal animals. Yep, Robbie was definitely the master of sneaking around, but I didn't want him to know I was making a valentine for Jessie. I would just tell him that I was making a secret valentine for my mom. Tomorrow at school we would make a super-secret plan.

CHAPTER 4

K-I-S-S-I-N-G

The next day at school I told Robbie I needed his help coming up with a super-secret plan.

"Of course I'll help you think of something," Robbie said, patting me on the back. "But not right now. Mrs. Wushy is looking this way."

"Listen carefully, everyone," said Mrs. Wushy. "Today we are going to decorate these bags for Valentine's Day." She held up a small white lunch bag.

"Mrs. Wushy, I don't think those bags are big enough for twenty valentines," said Chloe.

"Oh, I use these bags every year, and there is plenty of room for all of your valentines," Mrs. Wushy answered, smiling.

"Well, my valentines are huge, and I put a really fancy box of chocolates with each one."

"A whole box of chocolates?" said Max, licking his lips. "Yum!"

Chloe turned to Max. "You don't even deserve one. The only reason you're getting a box is because Mrs. Wushy said we had to give a valentine to everybody in the class."

"Well, every time I bite into one of those chocolates, I'll pretend it's your head," Max said, laughing.

"I am not going to put up with this behavior again today," Mrs. Wushy interrupted. "This is your last warning, you two. Next time, it's off to the principal's office. Do you understand?"

They both nodded their heads.

"Anyway, as I was saying, Chloe, these

bags are plenty big enough, but if someone's valentine does not fit, then you can just place it next to the person's bag."

"I can't believe she is going to give everybody a whole box of chocolates," I whispered to Jessie. "Those are really expensive."

"She thinks she's better than everyone else," Jessie whispered back. "She thinks if she gives people expensive stuff, then they'll like her."

"I don't really like her even if she does give us that stuff. She's always bragging too much, and she bosses everybody around."

"Yeah, I know. Well, you can't buy friends," Jessie said, squeezing my hand. "You're a really good friend, Freddy."

I could feel my cheeks getting hot. I was sure my face was as red as a tomato.

"Are you all right?" asked Mrs. Wushy. "Your cheeks are very red. Maybe you have a fever. I'd better send you to the nurse."

Oh, why did she have to say that? Now everyone in the class was looking at me. I was so embarrassed. "No, that's okay, Mrs. Wushy. I'm fine. It's just a little hot in here."

"I think he's turning red because his girl-friend is holding his hand," Max snickered.

Oh no! I didn't realize that Jessie was still holding my hand. I quickly let go of her hand. "She's not my girlfriend," I said.

"Freddy and Jessie, sitting in a tree, K-I-S-S-I-N-G!" Max sang loudly.

I wished I could make myself disappear. I'd never been so embarrassed in my life!

"Max, that is enough!" said Mrs. Wushy. "Just because two people hold hands does not mean they are boyfriend and girlfriend. You all are way too young to have boyfriends and girlfriends anyway. But boys can have girls who are friends, and girls can have boys who are friends."

"And Freddy is my good friend," said Jessie, sticking her nose in Max's face. "Do you have a problem with that?"

"Uh, no," Max said, grinning. "Just make sure you don't forget to give your little friend a kiss on Valentine's Day!"

"Max," said Mrs. Wushy, "you just earned yourself a trip to the principal's office. I am tired of your mouth. Right now!" she said, pointing to the door.

"B-b-but," Max stammered.

"Now!" Mrs. Wushy repeated, a little louder this time.

Max got up off the rug and stomped out the door in a huff. He didn't need anybody to show him the way to the principal's office. He had been there before.

"I'm sorry about that, boys and girls," said Mrs. Wushy. "As I said, we are all friends in this class. Boys can play with girls, and girls can play with boys, and there's nothing to be embarrassed about. In fact, when I was growing up, my best friend was a boy named Josh. We had lots of great adventures together."

I smiled at Jessie, and she smiled back.

"Now, let's get on with our project," Mrs.

Wushy continued. "These bags are blank, so you can decorate them any way you'd like. I put all kinds of fun materials on the tables that you can use. Just make sure you write your name in big letters on the front of the bag, so everybody knows it's yours. Once I give you a bag, you can find a seat and get started decorating."

Robbie and I sat down at a table together. I figured this was a good time to start making our plan. All I said was, "Now, about that plan," when Jessie came and sat down next to us.

"What plan?" asked Jessie.

"Freddy wants me to help him think of a way to sneak something up to his bedroom," said Robbie.

"What do you want to sneak up there?" Jessie asked.

"Um . . . I have to sneak some valentine

stuff up there, but I don't want my mom to see because I'm making her a secret valentine."

"Oooh, a secret valentine. That sounds super-cool," said Jessie. "I wish I were getting a secret valentine."

I smiled to myself.

"Anyway," said Robbie, "we have to help Freddy think of a plan."

"Why don't you put on a jacket that has really big pockets and hide everything in the pockets?" said Jessie.

"We did that once," said Robbie, "but this time Freddy has too much stuff he needs to carry. It won't all fit, and he can't make more than one trip."

I hit my forehead with the palm of my hand. "Think, think, think."

"Oh, I know," said Robbie. "Your mom is such a Neat Freak. She does laundry all the time. Tell your mom that you want to help her out by putting away your own laundry. When she gives you the stack of clean clothes, you sneak into the other room when she's not looking, and hide the stuff in between the clothes. Then you carry it all up to your room without anyone noticing!"

"What a great idea," I said, giving Robbie a high five. "You are a genius!"

"I know," he said, grinning.

"My mom will never suspect a thing. She'll just think I'm so sweet for helping her out around the house."

"That is a really good plan," said Jessie. "And I know your mom is going to love that special valentine."

I smiled at Jessie. "Oh, she'll like it. I know she will."

CHAPTER 5

Laundry Day

When I got home from school, I threw my backpack down in the kitchen and called, "Hey, Mom, where are you?"

"I'm in the laundry room, honey. Just finishing folding some clothes."

Bingo! This was my lucky day. I ran to find her. "Where's Suzie?"

"Hi, sweetie. She's over at Kimberly's. How was your day?"

"It was okay. We decorated our bags for the Valentine's Day party."

"That sounds like fun."

"Oh, and Max got sent to the principal's office . . . again."

"Really? What for?"

"He told the whole class that Jessie was my girlfriend, and he said that I should kiss her on Valentine's Day. I was so embarrassed."

"Why?"

"Because Jessie is just my friend. She's not my girlfriend. Why can't boys just be friends with girls?"

"They can. You know Max likes to tease people," my mom said.

"Well, Jessie is really tough. I bet she could beat up Max any day."

"Jessie is a very smart girl. Even though she is tough, she always uses her words. She stands up for what she believes in, but she never gets in a fight. That's why Max always gets sent to the principal's office, and Jessie doesn't."

"Yeah. She's really brave. I wish I could talk back to Max like that," I said.

"Max is just a big bully. Remember, I said that bullies only have power if you act afraid of them. Jessie never acts afraid."

"I'm glad she's my friend."

"Me, too."

"Is that all my stuff?" I asked, pointing to a pile of clothes.

"Yep. Are you looking for something?"

"No, I just thought I could help you carry it upstairs."

"Thanks, honey," my mom said. "That is so sweet of you to offer. Give me a minute, and we can take it all up."

"Oh, I can take mine by myself," I said.

My mom smiled. "You are getting to be such a big boy, Freddy."

I grabbed the stack of clothes and started out the door.

My mom stopped me. "Don't just put them on your floor. You need to put them in the drawers where they belong."

"Sure, no problem," I answered.

"I'll come help you as soon as I'm done here."

"No hurry," I said, smiling as I disappeared into the hall. I didn't have a lot of time to get the valentine stuff. I would have to work fast. My mom didn't have much more to fold.

I snuck into the kitchen and set the stack of clothes down on the table. My mom kept all the art supplies in a cabinet above one of the counters. There was no way I could reach it without standing on a chair. I would have to move one of the chairs from the kitchen table over and stand on that. Those chairs were really heavy to move. I would have to lift one because if I pushed it across the floor, my mom would hear the noise and come running to see what was going on.

I picked up a chair and grunted softly. Boy, was it heavy. As I started to walk across the kitchen, the chair kept bumping into my leg. It really hurt, but I just had to get those supplies.

I finally got to the counter and gently set the chair down. I climbed on top and reached up to open the cabinet. Rats! I was just a little too short. Now what was I going to do? I hit my forehead with the palm of my hand. "Think, think, think." I was running out of time.

Just then, a great idea popped into my head. I could get the phone book and put it on top of the chair. When I was little, my parents used to have me sit on the phone book so I could reach the kitchen table.

I stepped off the chair, quietly pulled open the drawer by the phone, and took out the phone book. Then I went and set it on top of the chair. I climbed up, stood on my tippy toes, and reached as high as I could. I pulled on the handle of the cabinet, and it sprang open so quickly I almost went flying off the chair. I grabbed the counter just in time. *Phew!* That was a close one.

I quickly pulled all the valentine supplies off the shelf and set them down on the counter. Then I slowly closed the cabinet and carefully climbed off the chair. I stopped for a minute to listen. Luckily, the last load of laundry was still drying, so my mom couldn't hear me over the sound of the dryer.

I put the phone book away, making sure I put it in the exact same spot where I found it. My mom is such a Neat Freak. She notices if even the tiniest thing is out of place. Then I carried the chair back to the table. My right leg was going to have a big bruise on it tomorrow.

I started to stuff the valentine things in between the layers of folded clothes. I hid the scissors and glue under my T-shirts, and I tucked the red paper, markers, stamps, and stickers in between my pants.

BUUZZZZZ. Oh great! That was the dryer. That sound meant the clothes were all

finished. My mom could fold clothes quicker than anybody. She'd be heading upstairs really soon. I had no time to waste.

I straightened up the pile of clothes, making sure none of the supplies were sticking out, and then I carefully picked the whole thing up and tucked the top layer under my chin. I didn't want to take the chance of anything falling out.

I tiptoed out of the kitchen and headed for the stairs. I had to walk slowly. I could barely see over the top of the pile, and I didn't want to trip and drop everything on the floor.

I had just reached the first stair when I heard her voice. "Freddy, is that you?" my mom called from down the hall.

Oh no! What if she caught me with the supplies? I would be in big trouble. Suzie and I were not allowed to have that stuff in our rooms because it made a big mess, and my mom didn't want us getting glue or markers on the carpet. I couldn't let her know I was hiding anything. I would have to act totally and completely normal.

"Yeah, Mom. It's me."

Just then my mom appeared, carrying her own pile of laundry. "I thought you had gone upstairs a long time ago."

Think fast. Think fast. "Uh, yeah. I was going to go straight up, but then my stomach was growling, so I stopped in the kitchen to get myself a snack."

"Why didn't you tell me you were hungry? I would have made you something to eat."

"Oh, that's OK, Mom," I said, smiling.

"Remember? I'm not a baby anymore. I want to do more things by myself now."

My mom smiled back. "I know, and I'm very proud of you, but that's an awful big pile of clothes you've got there," she said, reaching a hand out toward me. "Let me take half of those for you."

"No!" I yelled, turning quickly to the side so she couldn't touch my pile. The scissors almost slid out, but I caught them just in time and shoved them back in without my mom even noticing.

"My goodness, Freddy. I was just trying to help you."

"Sorry, Mom. It's just that I want to do things by myself, remember?"

"Well, all right. But be careful. I don't want you to trip going up the stairs."

"Don't worry, Mom," I said, taking a deep breath. "I'll be extra careful!"

CHAPTER 6

The Super-Secret Valentine

I thought I'd never make it up to my room without dropping all the stuff. I was so nervous because my mom was walking right behind me the whole time.

When we reached the top of the stairs, she said, "Here, honey, at least let me help you open your door."

I wasn't going to argue with her about that since I didn't really have a free hand, but then she followed me into the room. "Thanks,

Mom. I can do the rest myself. You can go now," I said over my shoulder.

"How about if I just separate it for you," she said, reaching for the pile one more time. "That will make it easier for you to put away."

I was starting to think I was going to get caught when the doorbell rang.

"Oh, that must be Suzie. Kimberly's mom was going to drop her off. I'll be back," my mom said as she ran out of my bedroom and down the stairs.

Lucky break. I set the pile down on my bed and closed my bedroom door. I didn't want anyone to see what I was doing. My mom would kill me for having art supplies in my room, and Suzie would tease me about having a girlfriend. This had to be super-secret.

I pulled the scissors, glue, paper, markers, stickers, and stamps out of the pile. Good thing that my shirts were clean! First, I put all the clothes away. Then I sat down on the floor to get to work.

This valentine had to be extra-special. I didn't want it to look like all the other valentines. Since Jessie was really into sports, I decided to make her a valentine in the shape of a basketball. I drew a big, round circle and cut it out. Then I drew the lines on it to make it look like a real basketball. Next, I cut out a heart to glue on top, but it came out crooked, so I cut another and another. Each one I crumpled up and threw on the floor. I wanted this valentine for Jessie to be perfect. I couldn't put a crooked heart on it. I was getting really frustrated.

All of a sudden there was a knock on my door, and the handle started to turn. My heart skipped a beat. I ran over to the door and leaned against it. I did not want anyone opening it. "Open up, Poophead!" Suzie screamed.

"Go away. I'm busy."

"I'm not going away until you give me my pencil. I have to do my homework, and I can't find my new pencil with the hearts on it. I know you have it."

"I do not!" I yelled.

"Yes, you do!"

"Why would I have a pencil with hearts on it? Just use another one. You have a gazillion pencils in your desk."

"I have to have the heart one! If you're not going to look for it, then I will," she said. Then she pushed on the door so hard that it flew open, and I fell right on my butt.

"Get out!" I yelled, scrambling to my feet, but it was too late. Suzie saw everything.

"Oh my gosh," she said, her eyes getting bigger as she looked around the room. "You are in such big trouble. Just wait till Mom sees this."

I slammed the door closed. That's just what

I didn't need. My mom couldn't see this! "Please don't tell her," I begged.

"Why not? You know you're not allowed to have glue and markers in your room," Suzie said, grinning. "You are so busted."

"If you keep my secret, then I'll . . . I'll . . . "

"You'll what? It better be good."

"I'll give you all of my conversation hearts."

"And every one of your chocolate kisses," Suzie added.

"All of my chocolate kisses? But those are my favorites!"

"Do we have a deal?" Suzie asked, holding up her pinkie for a pinkie swear.

"How about just *some* of my chocolate kisses?"

"It's all or nothing. Is it a deal or not?" Suzie asked. She was getting a little impatient.

"Deal," I said, as we locked pinkies. "Good. Now you can leave."

"Not so fast. I still don't have my heart

pencil," Suzie said. "And you still haven't told me what you're doing."

"Nothing."

"If it's nothing, then why do you have all the valentine stuff up here? You must be making a valentine for someone."

"Uh, yeah. I am."

"Who's it for?"

I couldn't tell her it was for Jessie, or she'd never stop teasing me.

"Oh, I know," she said, smirking. "It's for your girlfriend."

"How many times do I have to tell you I don't have a girlfriend?" I yelled.

I guess I yelled a little too loudly because my mom knocked on the door. "Freddy, is everything all right in there?"

I put my finger to my lips and stared hard at Suzie. Then I whispered, "If you tell, the deal is off!"

Suzie started to open her mouth, and I thought for sure she was going to tell on me, but she said, "Everything's fine, Mom. Freddy's just telling me a story."

"Well, OK, but you're supposed to be doing your homework, Suzie."

"I will in a minute. I'm just looking for my new pencil with the hearts on it."

"How about if I come in and help you look,

to speed things up?" my mom asked through the door.

"No! No! That's OK, we can find it," we both answered together.

"Two more minutes, Suzie, and then I'm coming in to get you."

"OK, Mom. I heard you. Two more minutes," Suzie answered.

Finally my mom walked away. I breathed a sigh of relief.

"Thanks for not telling on me, Suzie. You're the best big sister in the whole world."

"I know," she said, grinning.

I wanted her to get out of my room so I could finish the valentine. Maybe if I told her where the dumb pencil might be, she'd go look for it and forget about asking me who the valentine was for.

"Why don't you check the bathroom for

that pencil? I think I remember seeing it on the counter in there this morning."

"The bathroom? Why would I have a pencil in the bathroom?"

"I don't know, but you practically live in there. Maybe you took it in there with you because you were planning on taking it to school, and you didn't want to forget it."

"Are you sure?" she asked.

"Why don't you just go check," I said, shoving her out the door.

"It better be there," she called as she headed toward the bathroom.

I shut the door and looked at the mess in my room. It was only a matter of time before my mom came knocking again. I had to finish the valentine and get the mess cleaned up before she came back. I would hide the supplies under my bed until I could figure out a way of getting them back downstairs.

I sighed a big sigh. Making a super-secret valentine was hard work, but it was worth it. I couldn't wait to see the look on Jessie's face when I gave it to her on Friday.

CHAPTER 7

The Big Day

Valentine's Day finally arrived. I had been waiting all week, and it seemed as if it would never come. Every year, I loved getting all the candy and cards from my friends, but today was going to be extra-special because I was finally going to give Jessie the super-secret valentine.

I had decided I would give it to her at recess when no one else was looking. Maybe we could sneak behind the building where we hide from Max when he is chasing us. No one usually goes back there. I didn't want anyone else to know that I made her the valentine. Not even Robbie. This would just be our little secret. Jessie was really good at keeping secrets.

I got dressed and put on my pants with the deepest pockets. I didn't want to take any chances. If the card fell out of my pocket, then everyone would see it, and my whole plan would be ruined. I took the valentine out of my baseball-card box where I had been hiding it, folded it carefully, and stuck it deep down into my pants pocket. I really tried to push it down as far as it would go. Then I put on my red shirt (everyone in the class was supposed to wear something red today), hooked my lucky shark's tooth on my belt loop, and ran downstairs for breakfast.

Suzie was already at the table. Next to each of our plates was a valentine surprise. Mine was a little stuffed shark. He had a tag that said, "You are so cute I could eat you up! Will you be my valentine?" Suzie had a stuffed pink kitty cat with a tag that said, "You are purrrfect. Be mine." In between us was a big box of chocolates.

"Happy Valentine's Day, Freddy," said my mom and dad.

"Happy Valentine's Day to you, too. Can I eat one of these candies?" I asked as I started to open the box.

"When? Now?" asked my mom.

"Yeah."

"No," said my dad. "Close that box. You can't eat chocolate now."

"Why not?"

"Because they're for us to share," Suzie snarled, grabbing my wrist. "Get your grubby hands off the box."

"Let go of me, you little brat!" I yelled, trying to shake my hand free.

"Oh, for heaven's sake," said my mom. "This is supposed to be a day of love and kindness. Can't you two get along for one day?"

"Your mother has made you something very special for breakfast," my dad said. "Now let go of each other and sit down."

We both sat back down in our chairs, and my mom brought over two plates and set them in front of us.

"Wow! This looks yummy, Mom," I said. "What is it?"

"They're heart-shaped waffles with whipped cream and strawberries."

I smacked my lips. Then I stuck my finger in the whipped cream and licked it off. "Mmmmmmmm."

"Freddy," said my mom, "please use a fork. You're not a monkey."

"He sure looks like a baboon to me," Suzie said, laughing.

I got out of my chair and started jumping around and howling like a monkey. "OOOOO, AHHH, OOOOO, AHHH!"

"Stop it. Get away from me, Weirdo," Suzie said, waving her arms to shoo me away.

"But you said I was a baboon!" I answered, howling in her face.

"Mom, Dad," Suzie whined, "make him go away. He won't leave me alone."

"Freddy," said my dad, "go sit down. It's not time to play. You need to eat so you don't miss the bus. You still have to pack up your backpack."

"That reminds me," said my mom. "We have to put all the lovely valentines you made in your backpacks, so you can take them to school today. You both did such a nice job. I know your friends are going to love them."

"Oh, I know they will," I said, patting my pocket.

"I think mine are going to be the best in the class this year," Suzie said.

"You'd better get a move on," my dad interrupted. "It's getting late."

"Yes," said my mom. "You have a big day today. I know you wouldn't want to miss it."

Little did she know how big it really was.

CHAPTER 8

A Red Tomato

I couldn't concentrate in school because all I could think about was giving Jessie the valentine at recess. I kept going over the plan in my head. As soon as we went outside, I would tell her to meet me behind the building. Then when no one was looking, I would give her the super-secret valentine.

My thoughts were interrupted by Mrs. Wushy. "Freddy, do you know the answer?"

Robbie elbowed me in the side. "Freddy, wake up. Mrs. Wushy is talking to you."

"What, Mrs. Wushy?"

"I said, do you know the answer?"

"The answer to what?"

"To my question. You need to pay more attention and stop daydreaming, Freddy. I know you're excited about our party later, but right now we have to do some work. Does anyone know the answer to my question?" Mrs. Wushy asked.

"I do! I do!" Chloe said, waving her hand wildly in the air. She was dressed all in red. Her dress was red, her socks were red, her shoes were red, her hair ribbon was red, and, of course, she had painted her nails bright red.

Jessie leaned over and whispered, "Look, it's a talking tomato."

I had to bite my tongue to keep from laughing. If Mrs. Wushy had to speak to me again, then I might get a time-out and have to sit on the bench at recess. That would ruin everything. If I was benched, then I wouldn't be able to give Jessie the valentine.

"Yes, Chloe, what is the answer?"

"If I had seven valentines, and you gave me thirteen more, then I would have twenty valentines all together."

"Very good, Chloe," said Mrs. Wushy. "That is correct."

Chloe smiled and batted her eyelashes. "Thank you, Mrs. Wushy. I've been practicing a lot at home."

Max batted his eyelashes. "I've been practicing a lot at home," he mimicked.

Chloe turned to Max and glared at him. "Stop copying me."

"Stop copying me," Max mimicked again.

"I said stop copying me," Chloe said, almost in tears.

"I said stop copying me," Max repeated.

Mrs. Wushy let out a big sigh. "Max, that is

enough. Leave Chloe alone. If you bother her one more time, then you will not get to stay for the party this afternoon."

"That's not fair," Max groaned.

"Oh, yes. It's very fair," said Mrs. Wushy. "Now go sit in that chair over there and behave. This is your last warning."

Max went to sit in the chair, and he didn't say anything else the rest of the morning. I didn't blame him. Who would want to miss a fun party?

Finally, it was time for recess. My heart was beating really fast, and my palms were all sweaty. As we all started to walk out to the playground, I grabbed Jessie and whispered, "Meet me behind the building in our secret hiding place."

"Why?" she whispered back.

"Just go," I said.

Jessie went first, and I followed. I kept

looking around to make sure no one saw us go
back there. Max was chasing Chloe, so at least
he wasn't watching what we were doing.

When we got there, Jessie started laughing.

"What's so funny?" I asked.

"Oh, nothing," she said. "You're just acting
real funny. Why do you keep looking over
your shoulder?"

"Shhhh," I said. "I don't want anyone to
hear us back here."

"So, what's the big secret?"

It was now or never. I reached into my pocket and pulled out the valentine. "This is . . . this is, for you."

"What is it?" Jessie asked.

"Read it."

Jessie opened it up and read, " 'To Jessie, I really like being your friend. You are so cool. Will you be my valentine? From Freddy.' "

My heart was beating so fast I thought it was going to pop out of my chest. I could feel my cheeks getting redder and redder and hotter and hotter. Now I was the one who looked like a big red tomato.

"Of course I'll be your valentine, Freddy," she said.

"But we have to keep it a secret," I whispered, putting my finger to my lips. "I don't want anyone to know about this super-secret valentine. Don't talk about it to anyone."

"Why not?" she asked.

"Because," I said. "Just because."

"OK," Jessie said, giggling. "It will be our little secret." She pretended to zip her lips, lock them up, and throw away the key.

"Now, let's get out of here before Max finds us. I don't want people to know we were back here together. You go first."

Jessie started to walk away, but I grabbed her by the back of the shirt. "Wait, wait!"

Jessie turned around. "Now what?"

"Where's the valentine?" I asked.

"What valentine?"

"What do you mean, 'what valentine'?"

"I don't know what you're talking about," Jessie said.

"Yes, you do!" I said. "The super-secret valentine I just gave you."

"Oh, you mean the one I'm not supposed to talk about," Jessie said, laughing.

"Ha, ha. Very funny," I said. "Where did you put it?"

"I put it in a special hiding place," Jessie said, patting her pocket. "Don't worry. Your secret is safe with me."

"Thanks for being such a great friend," I said. Then I gave Jessie a little push. "Now get out of here before Max finds us!"

She turned and smiled at me and ran off. Two seconds later Max found me. "Well, lookie here," he said, smirking. "Look what I found. Baby Freddy. Valentine's Day must be my lucky day."

"Nope. It's mine," I whispered to myself and smiled. And then I took off running.

DEAR READER,

Valentine's Day is one of my favorite holidays. When I was little, my mom and dad always had a special surprise waiting for me at the breakfast table on Valentine's Day morning. One year when I walked into the kitchen, I saw a huge, stuffed bear sitting in my seat at the table. He was wearing a T-shirt that said, "You are beary sweet. Will you be my valentine?" I will never forget that.

I still love getting and giving cards and treats to my friends and family on Valentine's Day. I also love to eat all the chocolates!

I'm sure you have gotten some very special valentines. I'd love to hear about them. Just write to me at:

Ready, Freddy! Fun Stuff

c/o Scholastic Inc.

P. O. Box 711

New York, NY 10013-0711

I hope you have as much fun reading *Super-Secret Valentine* as I had writing it.

HAPPY READING!

Abby Klein

Freddy's Fun Pages

FREDDY'S SHARK JOURNAL

Dear Megamouth: Will you be my valentine?
THE KINDEST SHARKS:
PLANKTON-EATING SHARKS

The whale shark, the basking shark, and megamouth are three of the biggest sharks, but they eat plankton, some of the smallest living things in the sea.

Plankton-eating sharks have spongy filters or rows of thin bars in front of their gills. They are called rakers.

These big sharks take in huge mouthfuls of sea water, and their rakers act as nets to capture (trap) the plankton, which they then digest.

The plankton eaters are not aggressive and let divers swim close to them.

SUPER-SECRET
VALENTINE WORD SEARCH

Can you find these words in the word search?
The words may be hidden across, down,
and diagonally. Good luck!

CANDY   CARD   GLITTER

FLOWERS   STAMPS   MARKERS

RED   FRIENDS   STICKERS

HEART   DOILIES   LOVE

```
B  H  F  S  S  M  T  M  X  I  T  Y
C  G  P  K  G  A  T  D  T  K  D  A
G  A  N  H  A  R  U  R  Z  N  T  N
C  L  R  E  C  K  Y  Q  A  C  Y  S
Q  P  I  D  I  E  S  C  C  D  F  G
I  R  I  T  A  R  W  P  W  V  P  B
T  P  U  K  T  S  C  D  M  L  L  C
R  E  B  A  R  E  O  S  D  A  Y  K
A  S  D  N  E  I  R  F  K  R  T  C
E  I  P  B  L  E  L  O  V  E  H  S
H  K  Q  I  K  H  W  F  W  D  A  T
P  Z  E  C  D  D  L  R  S  Q  O  R
Q  S  I  F  L  O  W  E  R  S  J  C
E  T  K  R  Q  K  F  S  F  S  I  P
S  E  L  Q  N  G  O  I  N  G  D  H
```

VALENTINE'S DAY PUZZLE

How many different words
can you make from the words:

VALENTINE'S DAY

Lean

net

dave

vane

lend

lane

VALENTINE HAPPY-FACE WAFFLES

Would you like to make the special waffles that Freddy ate on Valentine's Day? You will need a heart-shaped cookie cutter.

INGREDIENTS:

♥ waffles ♥ strawberries ♥ whipped cream ♥

DIRECTIONS:

1. Have an adult help you make waffles.

2. Cut them out with a heart-shaped cookie cutter.

3. Use 2 strawberries for the eyes, one strawberry for the nose, and make a mouth with the whipped cream. You can also use the whipped cream to make hair.

4. Eat and enjoy! Happy Valentine's Day!

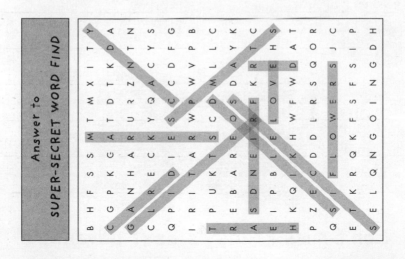

Have you read all about Freddy?

 Freddy will do anything to lose a tooth fast!

 Freddy has the best show-and-tell ever!

 Freddy's research makes big trouble!

Will Freddy beat Max the bully?

 Help! Does anyone have a magic spell for talent?

 Can Freddy make the vampire go away?

Yikes! How fast can Freddy learn to ride a bike?

Oh no! Freddy is afraid of ghosts and goblins!

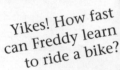 Can Freddy buy a Megalodon tooth?

Don't miss Freddy's next adventure!